Published by Knights Of
Knights Of Ltd, Registered Offices:
119 Marylebone Road, London, NW1 5PU

www.knightsof.media
First published 2023
001

Written by Nikesh Shukla
Text © Nikesh Shukla, 2023
Cover and internal art © Rochelle Falconer, 2023
All rights reserved
The moral right of the author and illustrator has been asserted

Set in Bembo Std
Typeset design by Sophie McDonnell
Typeset by Sophie McDonnell
Printed and bound in the UK

A CIP catalogue record for this book will be
available from the British Library

ISBN: 9781913311445

NIKESH SHUKLA

Illustrated by **ROCHELLE FALCONER**

KNIGHTS OF

For Rohit and Kian.

CHAPTER 1

You can hear them before you see them, thundering through the courtyard at full gallop: Vinay leading the pack, giggling like a terrified chicken, Musa running fast and focused, and Inua, leaping as if he hopes each stride will bring him closer to take off (one day, he will learn to fly). They're being chased by Nish, wielding two large canons,

each one attached to a canister of coloured water: one purple, one orange.

He is screaming for them all to *STAY CALM*, *stay calm* and *come back*.

Every passer-by is in the firing line. Vinay bumps into someone, Musa startles the postal worker, who drops all their mail, and Inua has to leap over a pushchair, like he's LeBron James.

Except, Nish knows what he is doing. He has cornered them all into a walled section of their estate's playground. There's no escaping.

Unless Inua can actually fly.

Vinay spins around so his back is against the wall. He holds out two peaceful hands, palms outstretched.

'Woah, easy there, fella, let's not do anything silly.'

Nish smiles as he takes aim.

'I don't make the rules,' he says.

'You literally do,' Musa says.

'It's Holi,' Nish replies. 'The festival of colours. And so, I'm just doing what needs to be done.'

Musa sticks a hand up.

'Yes, Musa,' Nish gestures to him with one of the canons.

'I'm going to get into so much trouble if I come home in purple clothes.'

Musa is wearing a gleaming white t-shirt that he takes extreme pride in. It is never dirty. *Ever.* Because they've all met his parents. They mean business. Also, as Musa once said, nothing fills him with confidence more than a crisp white t-shirt.

Nish ushers Musa over to him and hands him the orange canon.

'WHAT...' Inua shouts. 'That's not fair.'

'Time to learn how to FLY,' Nish shouts.

'What about me?' Vinay asks.

'Who do you think filled up the canons? Your mum,' Nish says. 'I think that means…'

Nish and Musa spray their canons in Vinay's direction, and he drops to his knees, like a fallen soldier in a war movie, his wrists to the sky like the heavens have forsaken him.

'Nooooooo,' he cries out, as coloured water splatters off him like slow motion ricochets of rainbow.

Inua tries to use this as his opportunity to escape and, as he runs away, Musa and Nish spray the water at him. Inua ducks into a forward roll, stacking his landing on the bumpy ground and tumbling with a crash, groaning as his back smacks against the ground. Nish and Musa stand over him, pointing their canons.

Inua bursts out laughing. 'Okay, you got me, you got me!'

Musa offers Inua a hand and pulls him to his feet. Vinay joins them and nudges Nish playfully.

'Happy Holi, boys,' he says, before snatching at Musa's canon, catching him off-guard and running off with it.

He swivels to face his three best friends. Musa holds his hands up. Vinay smiles, the power coursing through his veins.

'Listen,' Musa says. 'Think very carefully about what happens next.'

'Vinay,' they all hear shouted across the courtyard. Turning, Vinay sees his Papa ushering him over. 'Time to say goodbye to your Ba and Bapuji.'

Musa lets out a huge sigh of relief ... before Nish and Inua both point to three orange specks that pepper the chest of his once-gleaming-white t-shirt. He groans. *Bad vibes.*

Vinay stands between his mum and dad, Papa's arm around him as he smiles at Ba and Bapuji. They're going back to India for a while. They don't like the weather here. Or the people. Bapuji once told Vinay that everyone on the bus looks so sad; he wants to live somewhere where, even if they're not smiling, at least it's hot. It's better for Ba's asthma. Vinay's dad is about to drive them to the airport. Mum isn't going, she is way too pregnant. She can barely walk, and she can barely sit. Nothing makes her comfortable. Vinay's baby sister hasn't even been born yet and yet she's all anyone talks about.

Vinay says goodbye to Ba and Bapuji. He doesn't feel too sad, for two reasons. The first is, he's going to India at Christmas for a wedding, so he'll see them soon. The second: Vinay is getting their room.

A room of his own.

Musa, Inua and Nish come over to say goodbye. It's kisses and cuddles and a few tears from Ba (and from Bapuji too), and, as Papa drives them away to the airport and Vinay waves goodbye, everything in him is stopping him from running up the stairs and taking charge of his new domain.

'Come on then,' Inua says. 'Show us your new room.'

They all cheer and rush inside, pushing past Mum, who laughs at them all as they bound up three flights of stairs to Vinay's flat.

CHAPTER 2

Vinay stands in the middle of the small box room. Without a bed, it still looks tiny, but it is his, all his, and he doesn't care. He points around the room.

'I'm putting a bunk bed there,' he says, gesturing to one wall. 'And maybe my Arsenal poster there...' He points to the back of the door, as Musa and Nish, ardent Manchester United fans, let their displeasure show.

Inua, the basketball king, shrugs. He has no skin in this game.

Vinay talks them through where his stack of Marvel Annuals will go, and the incomplete sets of Lego they'd found in a charity shop and then argued over, as they tried to build the Death Star from a pile of mixed-up pieces. When all is said and done, he doesn't have a lot of stuff, but that's okay. As Vinay himself often says: 'I'm a kid. I've got time to accumulate stuff. I love stuff.'

'You going to sleep on the top bunk?' Nish asks.

'Of course,' Vinay replies, rudely, as if there has never, in the history of questions, been one with a more obvious answer. 'Why?'

'You're scared of heights,' he replies, laughing.

'It's a bunk bed, not Mount Kenya . . .'

'Don't you hate how the British keep saying they discovered Mount Kenya?' Inua says. 'Like all the Kenyans who live nearby just ignored that massive mountain and then the British came and were like, oh look, a mountain.' He shakes his head. 'I bet it wasn't even called Mount Kenya.'

'Kirinyaga,' Vinay says, and everyone looks at him like he's a genius. 'Dad's Kenyan,' he adds, to explain.

'When does the bunk bed arrive, Vin?' Nish asks.

'Tuesday,' Vinay replies, before stretching his arms around him and swirling around in a circle like he's on a mountain singing about how free he is. 'Mine,' he yells. 'All mineeee!'

He smacks his hand on something hard and the whole gang recoils from a tower of boxes and suitcases, filled with sarees and sherwanis and sheets and all sorts of nonsense, that do not belong in the bedroom of Vinay S.K. Patel Esquire.

'Well, that's all got to move,' he says.

Inua and Musa roll their imaginary sleeves

11

up and lift the top box off the teetering tower. It's heavy.

'How are sarees so heavy?' Nish asks, offering a steadying hand.

'All those sequins, I guess,' Vinay says.

Inua and Musa tumble the box to Inua, to Musa, to Inua and back to Musa, Nish wisely stepping backwards out of the way as they both drop the box. It slams down on the floorboards with enough of a thud to wake Godzilla. Inua and Musa stare at each other.

Rumble, rumble, rumble.

'Sorry,' Nish says, as everyone tries to identify the noise. 'Just hungry.'

'Come on,' Vinay says. 'Let's get all this nonsense out of my room.'

There's a knock on the door and then Vinay's mum enters, pregnant belly first, hands on hips, leaning backwards to try and keep her back straight.

'What was that noise?' she says. She sighs when she sees the fallen box of sarees.

They all point at each other, like they're all Spider-Man, each boy blaming everyone else. Mum laughs and shakes her head.

'Don't worry, when the wardrobes arrive all these boxes will fit on top of them.'

Vinay looks at her with a disgusted face, like someone has done the most garlic-iest of burps ever.

'On top?' he asks, gulping.

'Oh yes, definitely,' Mum says. 'We need two wardrobes now your cousin's staying with us. You'll be sharing a room with him. Isn't that exciting?'

Vinay's jaw drops. Inua pushes it back up with his hand.

'My cousin's what?'

Vinay repeats, like all the air in his lungs has leaked out and all that's left is despair.

'Snacks anyone?' Mum says, disappearing out of the room, a chaotic mess in her wake.

'I wonder if he'll take the top bunk,' Nish says, breaking the silence.

CHAPTER 3

Vinay is fuming. He had one whole day to enjoy the room on his own. One beautiful, brilliant day. And now he is spending it on the bus to the airport, sitting next to his mum; him reading silently, her reading out the voices of the different characters from his comic in a silly voice.

At first, he finds it annoying and pokes at Mum to stop until she giggles.

He doesn't want her to know how mad he is. Not only has he lost the most important thing in his life, but also, now he's spending the one day he had to enjoy it on the smelly bus, with all the people eating their smelly

16

sandwiches on their way to work. It's so hot and the bus stinks of egg mayo sandwiches.

Egg mayo sandwiches are the worst sandwiches. When the thing in the sandwich is softer than the bread around it, it's no good. Also, who likes sandwiches really? Vinay hates Thursdays at school because they make him eat sandwiches. You know what's better than sandwiches? *Rice.*

Inua's mum always says, 'There's rice at home,' whenever they're out and he says he's hungry. He always groans when she says it, because he wants an ice cream or a bit of chocolate or something. Vinay always thinks, *great, Inua's mum knows what's important: rice. I love rice.* Vinay would eat rice for every meal if he could. The best days are when they get to have pava for breakfast, then rice and vegetarian meatballs at school and then rice with the dhal at home. And if Vinay is really lucky, he will finish it off with a delicious bowl of rice and yoghurt, seasoned with some chaat powder. *That's the best dessert ever,* he thinks.

He gets so mad when people are like, 'let's eat sandwiches for lunch'. He always thinks: *Nooo, there is all this deliciousness you could add to a bowl of rice, and instead you're choosing two yucky thin slices of white foam and a lump of moist cheese in the middle? Come on, why do you hate yourself?*

Vinay gets mad at sandwiches in his head, and it means he's not mad at Mum for a few minutes. He doesn't want to be mad at her. He understands how much family means to her.

Vinay's mum looks at him and smiles, stroking her belly.

'I know you're angry at me,' she says.

'No, I'm not,' he shouts, quite loudly.

(Like an angry person might.)

'You certainly sound it,' Mum says, sighing, slightly embarrassed that other people can hear his rudeness in public. 'And don't talk to me like that, just because we're in a public place it won't stop me from shouting back. I don't care if anyone thinks I'm being horrible to you.'

'Sorry,' Vinay says, jutting out his bottom lip, shaking a little, trying to not cry.

'I know you were looking forward to having your own room,' she tells her son. 'But your cousin Nikesh is family. Okay? Treat him like family.'

★★★

Vinay has only met Nikesh once, on the phone. They were both handed the phone and told to get to know each other. They each asked how the other was. Nikesh talked about how much he loved cricket and Vinay talked about why Arsenal was the best team in the world, and then their mums took the phones back and marvelled at well the boys got on. Now, he's coming here, and Vinay is annoyed that this guy hasn't even arrived and is already taking his stuff. His room. Vinay is getting the top bed, no matter what, he decides.

When they arrive at the airport terminal, Vinay helps his mum off the bus and holds her hand as they walk slowly into the airport, following the signs for Arrivals. Vinay is amazed to see so many people around him, walking hand in hand, carrying suitcases, rushing past him, taking their time to say a lingering, sad goodbye, and eating, everyone seems to be eating.

They wait by a barrier. Vinay leans against it, his eyes on a set of white sliding doors that occasionally open and reveal people arriving. Where are they arriving from? It could be anywhere in the world, or they could just really like standing behind doors, and jumping out, shouting, *I've arrived!*

Everyone looks happy to arrive.

Vinay notices Nikesh when he appears, the only person not smiling, accompanied by a member of the airport staff. He looks small and scared. He has wide shoulders and stiff arms, and his hands are clenched into his pockets. He wears glasses and has long hair, swept into a messy bun. He does not want to be here.

They lock eyes and Vinay calls out Nikesh's name. Either he doesn't hear him initially, or he doesn't recognise his cousin, but it takes a while for Nikesh to turn to Vinay. He still doesn't smile. The airport staff member walks over to Vinay and Mum joins him. She has identification things to show who she is. And before long, the three are left alone together. In the airport.

As they sit at a café near the exit and Vinay chews through a croissant, he stares at Nikesh's pain au chocolat, sitting in front of him, uneaten.

'How was your flight?' Mum asks Nikesh.

He stares ahead of him. Not at his plate and not at Vinay, but somewhere in between.

'Fine,' he mumbles.

'Are you not hungry?'

'I'm fine,' he says again.

'Are you going to eat that pain au chocolat?' Vinay asks, grinning, his hands already reaching across the table, and grabbing the pastry before Nikesh can say anything.

Nikesh, quick as a rabbit spotting a fox, pulls the pastry back out of Vinay's loose grip, slamming it into his plate.

'That's mine,' he says.

Vinay looks at his mum, who is checking her phone and missing the entire interaction, then back to Nikesh.

'You're not eating it,' Vinay says.

'Neither are you,' Nikesh says. 'Because it is mine.'

Vinay smacks his hand to his head, as if to say 'What is this nonsense? Just give me the pain au chocolat, food waste is a serious issue.'

'Come on, let's go,' Mum says, putting down her mug of herbal tea and gripping the armrests of her chair to help her stand up.

Nikesh jumps to his feet and helps her to stand, even though she keeps saying 'don't worry beta'. He looks at Vinay the whole time. Vinay picks up Mum's bag and she grabs his chin and talks to him in that voice where she sounds calm, but she is a bit annoyed.

'Don't treat me differently,' she says. 'You know I hate that.'

'Sorry Mum,' Vinay says in a slow, deep voice, and she releases him before ruffling his hair.

'Right,' she says, turning to Nikesh. 'Let's get you back to your new home.'

'Where will I be sleeping?' Nikesh asks.

'Oh, don't worry,' Mum says. 'You won't be by yourself. You'll have a lovely snug room to share with your cousin.'

Vinay smiles at Nikesh, a peace offering, until he notices that the pain au chocolat is still on the table as they start to walk away.

Vinay goes to grab the pastry, but it's cleared away by a barista before he can get to it. He runs after the barista and nabs the pastry off the tray, shoving it into his hoodie pocket. He mutters a cheeky word to himself about Nikesh, about the lack of chocolate in his system, about wasting food, about his room, his beautiful room.

He's so annoyed that he squeezes the pain au chocolat in his pocket until it explodes.

CHAPTER 4

'It's not very big,' Nikesh says, dropping his backpack on the floor.

Before Vinay can say or do anything, Nikesh has jumped onto the ladder that takes him up to the top bunk, where he shouts, 'Dibs!'

'Huh?' Vinay replies.

'Dibs,' Nikesh says. 'That's what you say when you're claiming something for yourself. You shout tax, cos you just taxed it. Have you never heard that before?'

'No,' Vinay says, flatly. He does not agree.

It takes Vinay an extra few seconds to realise what is happening, and when he does, he stamps over Nikesh's bags and grabs the ladder: hauling himself up, screaming with rage, flakes of pain au chocolat trailing out of his pocket.

'Wait a minute,' he says. 'The top bunk is mine. It's not yours to tax.'

'Is that right?' Nikesh says, before kicking out with his bare feet at Vinay.

His big toe manages to snag a nostril, and it tickles Vinay so much he laughs and loses grip of the ladder. He falls backwards to the ground.

He slams his back into the floor and cries out in pain.

'Ow, ow, ow,' he says. 'That's not fair. I'm telling Mum.'

'Don't forget to tell her that I called dibs on the top bunk,' Nikesh says, laying down spread-eagled on the bed.

★★★

In the kitchen, Vinay's mum is making rotlis, sitting at the stove, on a stool Dad brought home from outside a restaurant near work for Ba. It was broken, but he managed to fix it. He always says don't ask him how he did it, but Vinay knows his secret because he helped his dad fix it. Let's hope that gaffer tape is strong because otherwise, Mum is going over . . . and it won't be pretty.

'Mum,' Vinay says, nearly in tears because he's so frustrated, and also, he landed on that funny bit in the middle of your back where your tailbone meets your bottom and it's surprisingly painful.

'Yes, darling,' Mum says, looking up at him from where she is resting her head on her arms, as she flips rotlis robotically.

'Nikesh took the top bunk.'

'Oh, lovely, that's so nice of you to give it to him. You're very kind.'

'No, you don't understand,' Vinay says. He is so frustrated, it's like his head might roll off his body. Except, it would roll towards his mum and, knowing how unsteady that stool is, she'd go over in a hot second. (*Hopefully away from the stove*, he thinks.)

Vinay watches as she uses fingertips

seemingly impervious to heat to turn over the rotli. *The tongs are right there, dude! Use them! Save your poor fingers.* Vinay stares at his own fingers.

'What don't I understand?' his mum asks, breaking his trail of thought.

'I wanted the top bunk. It was mine. I earned it.'

'Listen, darling,' Mum says, sitting upright and offering her hands to Vinay to grab. He does so, even though she's doing her famous 'trying to make him feel better' voice. 'Your cousin is in a very sad way, okay? Things are tough at his home with just his dad to look after him, and his mum no longer with us. My sister. Now, I said I would look after your cousin for a bit. Because it's the right thing to do. Even though our family is about to get bigger, we cannot turn our backs on the family we already have. Can we?'

'But—' Vinay starts to say.

'But nothing,' Mum says. 'He is your cousin. Your bhai. And I would expect you to treat him as such, okay, my darling?'

'Okay,' Vinay says, gulping, choking down tears.

He feels conflicted. Because much as he knows how sad Nikesh's life has been, he still has his own hopes and dreams to think of. And why should he give them up?

He realises that there is only one thing for it. He needs to assemble the council for advice.

'I'm going to see my friends,' he says to his mum, and she nods.

'It's dinner time soon,' she says. But it's too late; Vinay is out of the door.

CHAPTER 5

The council den is not easy to find. That's why they chose it. It's in Inua's back garden. But it's a *secret* back garden that backs on to the train tracks. Inua's mum's second floor flat has some steps outside the back door, leading down to an alleyway that takes you to the

WARNING!
Proceed at your own risk...

end of the ground floor flat's garden. Here, you'll find a swampy, muddy wasteland, with a tree obscured in the corner. Here, in the tree, is where their den is.

Musa noted that the constant noise of the tube, taking people into and out of the city for work and stuff, would be enough noise cover for the boys to talk freely. It's a Saturday afternoon, so Musa is bound to be there with Nish, listening to one of the various sports on the radio. Meanwhile, Inua will be feigning interest, drawing superheroes in notebooks and occasionally asking questions about different players. Even though he says he doesn't care about football or cricket or tennis or rugby or anything that's not NBA or WNBA basketball, he has still absorbed all the players' names, league standings and manager's foibles; he knows more than he lets on. He just doesn't want Musa or Nish to feel like they won him over.

Vinay arrives to the sound of Nish cheering as someone hits a six. You can hear the clack of the bat against the ball, and the crowd goes wild, and the commentator goes wild, and Nish goes so wild that Vinay can hear the branches shake.

'Here he is,' Musa says, as Vinay clambers up the tree to the slowly-rotting pallet that slices neatly down the middle of it.

'Hey boys,' Vinay says, spudding his friends.

Inua is up on his feet as Vinay sits cross-legged.

'What did you do about the bedroom? Did you mark your territory?'

'Yeah, Vin, did you wee around the top bunk like a lion?' Nish adds.

Vinay shakes his head.

'I need some advice,' he says.

Everyone stops what they're doing. Nish turns the radio off. The train rumble is now louder. The wind rustles in the summery shake of the trees. Everything else is quiet and still.

'Okay, so listen, I think my cousin is evil,' Vinay says.

He pulls out the squashed pain au chocolat from his pocket.

'Mum bought this for him at the airport and he wasn't going to eat it, and I went to grab it and he fought me 'til I dropped it.'

'Are you going to eat it?' Inua asks, and Vinay hands it to him.

Inua takes a bite. 'It's stale,' he adds.

'Wait, why do you have it if he made you drop it?' Musa asks.

'I grabbed it as we were leaving. I didn't want it to go to waste,' Vinay says. 'But listen, it gets worse.'

'Worse than stale pain au chocolat,' Nish says, his fingers to his chin like a detective on TV. 'Tell us more, young man.'

'He grabbed the top bunk. Just took it. With no discussion. And when I stormed the bunk to reclaim what was mine? He kicked me off.'

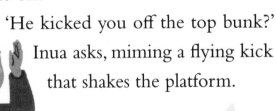

'He kicked you off the top bunk?' Inua asks, miming a flying kick that shakes the platform.

POW!!

'An actual kick or he kicked you off, like he said, no this is mine?'

'Actual kick.'

'Actual kick?'

'Yes. Actual kick.'

'Damn,' Inua says.

Musa is silent, which means he's coming up with the best approach for this. Musa is a man of peace. He knows how to make everyone work out what they want and come together for a compromise. He loathes arguing for the sake of it and shuts it down as soon as it happens. He rarely loses his temper.

Vinay asked him once what he was like when he was angry. And he repeated the famous Incredible Hulk line about how you wouldn't want to see him when he's angry, and everyone laughed, and Nish said, 'Yeah, Musa never gets angry, he just gets everyone to come together'.

'What do you want to happen?' Musa asks.

'I want the top bunk.'

'And so does your cousin, correct?' Musa says.

'Yes.'

'And he's here to stay. And given the layout of your flat, there is nowhere else for him to stay. You need to work something out. And it's a solution where both of you are a little happy and also, both of you don't get exactly what you want.'

'Classic Musa compromise incoming,' Nish says, laughing and laying back down, with his hands folded under the back of his head.

'Really?' Vinay says. 'Are you sure?'

'It seems to me like we need to talk to him and work out a rotation system. So you both share the top bunk. All you have to work out is how often you swap?'

Vinay thinks about it.

Inua crouches down between them. 'I disagree, Mus,' he says. 'I think Vinay needs to summon the laws of the wild here. Show his cousin who is boss and whose territory this is!'

'I'm not weeing around anything!'

'Fine, but you're going to lose,' Inua says. 'Call me when you're ready to get your hands dirty.'

Vinay thinks about the two solutions, then looks at Nish.

'What do you think, Nishant?' he says, using Nish's full name – which is how you get his attention, because his brain immediately thinks a parent is in the room.

Nish opens his eyes and says what he usually does: the easiest solution, the one no one actually wants to take.

'Why don't you just talk to him, cousin to cousin, and see how he's feeling? It's probably as weird a situation for him as it is for you?'

'Nah, you need to kick him,' Inua says, and everyone laughs.

As they're laughing, Musa fixes Vinay a look like, *you know I'm right, diplomacy is the only way. Choose love. Choose peace.*

In the silence that follows, Vinay high-fives Musa.

'Okay,' he says. 'I'll try it your way.'

'That's a mistake,' Inua murmurs, before jumping down from the tree to practise his kicks.

CHAPTER 6

Vinay asks his friends to accompany him. He feels better knowing that they're by his side. They've been there for him through everything, all the difficult things as well as all the good stuff. Like, they were all present the day he scored the goal he will remember

the rest of his life, where everything played out like a game of FIFA: the cross from Musa on the wing, arching perfectly towards Vinay, standing at the edge of the area, unmarked because he had burst from the back into space, undetected. The way his foot connected with the ball, a perfect volley that was a mixture of luck, instinct, precision and power, that sent the ball, towards the left corner of the goal, low and hard and out of reach of the goalkeeper (in this case: Nish).

They were also there the day he failed a spelling test. He didn't need the results to tell him how badly he had done. He knew while the test was happening, and he tried his best, but he just didn't understand what was going on.

They were also there when his dad had a fall at work and had to go to hospital. They all rode on the bus with Vinay and his mum.

His crew. His council.

Vinay and the council walk through his flat, almost like they are in slow-motion with a heavy funk beat playing. Actually, Vinay is just nervous – he hates conflict – and is taking his time getting to his bedroom.

Inside, it's dark. The curtains are closed, and the lights are off. There is some shuffling on the bed and the sound of snoring that was like a joke shop recording; it almost sounded fake.

'Nikesh?' Vinay asks, and some snuffles and snorts greet him.

Vinay looks at Inua, Nish, and Musa,

who are standing there awkwardly. Inua mimes a flying kick and Vinay shakes his head. Nish squeals with laughter.

They hear groaning from the bed as Nikesh rises, a duvet monster groaning scarily.

'Who is being loud?' he booms.

There is silence as the boys look at Vinay, willing him to answer. It takes Inua pushing Vinay forward before he utters, 'It's me, your cousin. Vinay.'

'The one you stole the top bunk from,' adds Inua, choosing chaos.

Nikesh uncovers himself and smiles in the darkness. You can see the glimmer of saliva against his teeth.

Musa, wanting a proper civilised discussion, opens the curtains. The light of the midday summer sun pours into the room, streaming directing into the backs of everyone's eyes and making them all squint.

'We need to have a talk,' Musa says. 'Not here. In the disputed territory. Outside. In the courtyard. On neutral ground.'

'Who are you all anyway?' Nikesh asks, rubbing his eyes, taking in this crew of boys. One ready to fight, another ready to negotiate, and another ready to cut him down to size with a well-timed, well-observed joke.

He processes their differing energies and leans his back against the wall to consider his moves.

Vinay says, 'These are my friends. Inua, Musa, Nish. My best friends. Listen, see you outside in five minutes.'

★★★

The boys stand in a line, twenty metres back from the front door of the building, watching and waiting for twenty minutes. When Nikesh emerges, his hair is damp and padded from what looks like a shower, and there's a slice of toast hanging in his mouth, smeared with chocolate spread, his hands in his pocket. He looks like he doesn't have a single care in the world; least of all, this peace brigade trying to broker some calm on the bunk bed.

Nish regards Nikesh's outfit and offers him some applause.

'That is a sick Spidey t-shirt. I've seen other people wearing it, but it looks so sick on you,' he says.

It takes Vinay a second to see the t-shirt. It is basically Spidey's top, but short-sleeved.

It's red, webbed, and blue at the sides, with the spider on the heart.

'I have a t-shirt just . . . like . . .' Vinay starts to say, before the realisation hits him like one of Inua's flying kicks. 'That's mine,' he shouts, losing his temper, his sense of self, his composure.

Vinay launches himself against Nikesh, fists raised, ready to fight, ready to punch him, and Nikesh smiles, almost as if this is exactly what he wanted. Before Vinay can reach him, Musa steps between them and acts as an immoveable blockade that stops Vinay dead in his tracks.

'That's not how we do things,' Musa says, and Vinay understands, remembering himself. 'Stay on target.'

'That's my t-shirt,' he says to Nikesh, and Nikesh shrugs.

'It was in my wardrobe, so I guess it's mine now actually,' Nikesh replies.

'Why are you being so mean to me?' Vinay says. 'We've only just met and we're sharing a room and . . .'

He stops himself, remembering Musa's suggestion. It's time to negotiate. He sits down on the floor, cross-legged, and pats at the space next to him. Musa crouches next to him. Inua circles behind them, stalking the circle. Nish plonks himself down on the floor, one knee to the floor, the other bended as a rest for his arm. He steadies himself with a hand on the floor.

Nikesh views this semi-circle with suspicion and sits down tentatively, his legs straight out in front of him, one foot over the other, his palms flat behind him keeping him upright.

'We need to talk,' Vinay says.

'Is this why you brought all your buddies? To try and scare me?'

Vinay looks at his friends and is suddenly embarrassed that maybe it looks like he's trying to be a tough guy, showing up with his crew, ready to throw down if he doesn't get what he wants.

'No,' he says. 'It's not like that. We need to discuss the rules of the bedroom. Our shared bedroom. I had all of these plans for it, and now you've moved in I want to make sure that we get along and make it the space we both want it to be.'

'You know, I've never had my own bedroom,' Nikesh says, smiling sweetly.

'Neither have I,' Vinay replies. 'That's why I was so excited.'

'I've never even had my own bed,' Nikesh says. 'Those gadlos my parents had were so uncomfortable, and Dad snores so badly, and so did Mum, when . . .' He stops talking, almost as if he's said too much.

'I have a suggestion,' Vinay says. 'A compromise, if you will. A scenario where we both get what we want, and both have to give a little to each other.'

'I'm listening,' Nikesh says, and this makes Vinay smile. Musa was right. All he needed to do was just reason with him and offer a solution that works for both of them.

'Maybe we take it in turns to have the top bunk. And we organise everything else in half. So, you have half the wardrobe and half the drawers, and half the wall space to hang up any poster you want. And look, if we ever want to borrow each other's clothes, then feel free, just check and ask.'

Vinay looks at Musa who nods, sagely, like this is exactly the right move. It gives Vinay a little shiver to know how proud his friend is of him.

'Interesting,' Nikesh says, looking off to the side.

A football bounces nearby. Nish leaps to his feet to kick the ball and return it to the lads from the top floor, the ones he is desperate to play with. So desperate is he, that he mistimes his step into the ball, and when he kicks it, he's too quick: the ball bounces under him. Quickly, to rescue him, Inua picks it up, throwing a perfect arching three-pointer back towards the game.

The ball gets stuck in the tree.

As the lads shout at Inua to go get it, he sits down next to Vinay, suddenly *very* interested in the negotiations.

'So, it's a deal?' Inua says.

'Shall we say a month each?' Vinay says. 'You can have the first month as a show of good faith from me.'

'What Vinay is trying to say is,' Musa says, interrupting. 'He's a good guy, you're a good guy, why don't you both be good guys together?'

'It's a good suggestion,' Nikesh says, without moving. 'The trouble is, I own the top bunk now. And if Vinay bhai wants to use it, he can pay me rent.'

'What?' Vinay says, looking around in disbelief.

Nikesh jumps to his feet and leans in close to Vinay.

'See you later, cousin,' he says, walking back towards the entrance of the block of flats.

'Wow,' Inua says. 'That really did not work.'

'No,' Musa says, sighing, heavily; not because his plan failed, but because he knows what this means. It means choosing chaos.

'He really is an evil man,' Nish says.

'Hey,' Vinay snaps, looking at his friend. 'That evil man is my cousin.'

CHAPTER 7

Vinay tries to read one of his favourite football programmes to help get him to sleep. It has a match report for a North London derby, and Vinay has read it so many times he can practically see the entire match play out across the springs of the bunk bed above him. He didn't even go to the match. He found it on a bus once. Someone had left it on a seat, and he kept it as a sign that one day he would be able to go to the Emirates Stadium and see his beloved Arsenal destroy the other North London team. (The team he dare not name.)

The mattress shakes every now and then,

as Nikesh tosses and turns above him. They haven't spoken since negotiations broke down. The boys all went to play football against the lads afterwards. Vinay put in a lacklustre performance, letting himself get nutmegged a couple of times and losing concentration during a stint in goal – letting in a couple of sitters. And then it was dinner, which was eaten in front of an IPL match

that Vinay's dad and Nikesh cheered along to. Mum was in bed, listening to a true-crime podcast with her eyes closed. So, Vinay sat at the table by himself, unable to concentrate on the match being played, even though it was going to decide the league standings.

Vinay listens to the silence. He had hoped for a room where he wouldn't have to shift around to the sounds of his father's snoring and his mother's sighing and both of their tossing and turning. He'd hoped for silence. But now he has the movements of Nikesh to contend with.

He thinks he can hear Nikesh crying, sniffling, sucking up snot into his nose.

'Are you okay?' he asks.

'Leave me alone,' comes the strained reply, and he knows he has caught his cousin in an awkward moment.

Vinay is dreaming about
being able to fly. He is
swooping down and
around a big tree-stacked
mountain, filled with dangerous paths
and rope bridges, and he has his hands by
his side. He can hear moaning and crying
and screaming from the path so he swoops
around the mountain looking for the source
of the upset; maybe he's not too late, he
can save whoever it is who needs saving.

Vinay realises, when he cannot see
anyone in distress, that he is dreaming and
the screaming and crying and moaning is
coming from the room he's in. Worrying his
cousin might be in danger, he forces himself
awake, gulping in a huge gasp of air. The
air in his room is cooler than in his dream
and everything is still, but it is dark, and in
the dark, with the slight frosting of light

from outside his window, he pulls himself up, calling out his cousin's name.

Jumping out of bed, Vinay thrusts two feet to the ground, but it's like his legs are dead and he cannot move at all. He falls to the floor, onto his face, putting his arms out in front of him, but they feel like they're glued together. And then there is a gurgle and splash of water as he is doused in something cold. Not knowing what's happening, gulping, flexing his limbs, panicking, calling out Nikesh's name, he falls to the floor and rolls over, his legs and arms useless, his ankles and wrists throbbing, his face and hair soaking wet.

Suddenly, there is a light on, and he squints as a hulking darkness creeps over him. He blinks and blinks his eyes open. He realises that it is his cousin, standing over him, wearing his Arsenal kit.

'I will say this only once,' Nikesh says. 'Next time you want to try and embarrass me in front of your friends, remember that you live in my home, in my bunk bed, and whoever has the top bunk is king.'

Vinay looks down at his hands and legs and realises that they've been tied with his school ties.

'Untie me,' he shouts. 'It hurts.'

'Get one of your friends to help you,' Nikesh says, turning the light off.

In the darkness, Vinay hears his cousin shuffle over him and up the ladder onto the top bunk.

'Untie me,' Vinay shouts again, hearing a shush from the next room, followed by a curt 'go to bed' shouted by his mum.

He lies there, feeling useless and pathetic, unsure of what to do, until he starts to rub his wrists together. Something starts to loosen, and he is finally able to pull a hand free.

CHAPTER 8

The next day, Vinay is unnecessarily grumpy with everyone. He is tired, so his patience is short. He shouts at his toast for burning. He shouts at his toothbrush for falling out of his hands when his eyes flicker and he starts to drift off in front of the mirror. He shouts at his feet for being too sweaty when he struggles to get his socks on as quickly as he can. This is moments after he has shouted at a clock for telling him he is running late. He is terse with Nish for being later than he was for the den meeting, even though Nish is always late. He then hits the tree when a stump of a branch snags his t-shirt, enough to give him a fright that it's torn. It's his favourite t-shirt. His mum found it in a charity shop. It has the Arsenal 2012/13 season team photo on it: obviously the best year. *Obviously.*

'Vin,' Musa asks. 'Are you okay?'

Just being asked if he is okay is enough for Vinay to burst into tears. He tells them about the horror of last night. Of being woken up scared, of his trapped limbs, of being numb and in pain, of the bowl of water, of being too wired to fall back asleep, of the almost comically loud snoring of his cousin. His friends look on in horror, except Inua, who nods like he knew it would come to this.

'I knew it would come to this,' he says.

'Let me tell you a story about the scorpion and the frog . . .

★★★

There's a big monsoon storm approaching, and the scorpion needs to get across the river to safety. All the animals who can swim are terrified and say no to helping him. Fair enough, he's a scorpion.

'You're a scorpion,' they all tell him.

And he's like, 'Geezers, listen to me, I too am scared, of dying in this monsoon. Do you not possess in your heart any amount of the animal kingdom version of humanity?'

And the animals are all like, 'Nah, we're animals. Only the strong survive.'

So, the scorpion is freaking out, right, and just, totally getting itself ready for death. A hero's death in the rain. Then it sees a frog, about to jump into the water and swim across. The scorpion runs over to the frog and corners it.

'Take me across,' it shouts.

The frog is like, 'Dude, are you kidding me? You're a scorpion. See you never, cos you're going to get wiped out in this monsoon storm in like thirty seconds.'

And the scorpion pleads with the frog, and sets out a compelling case, saying it would be silly for it to harm the frog, cos otherwise it would drown. And when it gets to the other side, it'll be so grateful, it'll just bounce and do what it's going to do.

And so, the frog goes, 'Okay fine. But listen, any funny business and you're done.'

So, the scorpion jumps on the frog's back and they start swimming across.

And you know what? It's totally fine, for the most

part. They talk, and they found out they have lots in common, and maybe in another life, they could've been friends. As they approach the bank, the scorpion can't hold it in anymore and it raises its tail. You see? It's in its nature to do what it's going to do.

So, it goes to sting the frog and teach it a lesson about nature vs nurture, and the rules of the jungle and all that, but the frog shouts, 'Now, boys, now!' And the frog kicks up its back legs, shooting the scorpion over its head, splashing it into the water, as the frog's boys all emerge from the marshes.'

'Wait, that's not how the story goes,' Vinay says.

It's lost in the heartily deep chuckle of an appreciative Musa, loving the remix of this classic story.

'The boys jump out of the marshes, and you know what? They are not mucking about. They splash about the scorpion, and make it wavy and the frog treads water in front of the drowning scorpion, and says, 'You were saying?'

And the scorpion, spluttering is, like, 'Rescue me,' and the frog goes, 'If I get you to land, you disappear, I never hear or see from you again,' and the scorpion is like, 'Yes, sure, anything, whatever you want.'

And the frog says, 'I don't believe you, you're a scorpion. I'll leave you here, and you either learn to swim and you remember my face, or you drown and the last thing you remember is that you tried to finish me off when I showed you a kindness. Yeah?'

And with that, the frog swims to the shore and hangs out with its boys and just lives his best life and the scorpion, well, who knows what happened, but the frog never thought about him again.'

★★★

Inua finishes the story, kneeling, arm on knee, his friends in a circle around him. There is a silence: he has such a beautiful way of telling stories. No matter how long they are, his friends always listen.

'Um,' Nish says. 'That was . . . an incredibly dark story. What's the moral? Leave all scorpions to die?'

Inua laughs. 'No, of course not. When the scorpion reveals its true nature, you show it that it may think it has the upper hand. But actually, it was always you. Because the scorpion moves alone. You have your crew. And that, my friend, is why you will win.'

'So what are you suggesting?' Vinay says.

'Gather round,' Inua says. 'And let us choose chaos together.'

CHAPTER 9

Inua's plan is simple: make him want to leave. Make the choice his and his alone. Because then he won't want to come back, and Vinay won't take any blame. Inua's plan is simple, sprawling and chaotic. It is basically to make the environment hostile.

'Like the government made the country for refugees like my parents,' Musa quips when Inua says his plan.

Everyone laughs. Nish pats Musa on the back, to remind him that, as much as they all laugh, they know how grim the whole thing is.

'Are you sure you don't just want to ask

if he's okay?' Nish asks again, but it's dismissed by everyone, even Musa, the one who never chooses chaos.

'Okay, so we have to show Nikesh how dangerous the top bunk is, but also the floor is lava, and the wardrobe is a black hole in space. But it doesn't stop there, because the food being served is not as good as home, and the courtyard is like a battlefield in a world war where all hope is lost, and school, well, don't worry about school, we have a long, hot summer ahead of us.'

Inua pauses, to look at his friends, who are giving him the look. A look he doesn't quite understand.

'What's up?' he says.

'You're an evil genius,' Nish says. 'Absolutely diabolical.'

Inua swells with pride.

'This doesn't feel like bullying, does it?'

Vinay asks. 'I worry this feels like bullying.'

'He started it,' Inua says, under his breath.

'I think what Inua is trying to say,' Musa says, taking a stance, 'is that diplomatic solutions have fallen down. And so, maybe we speak to him in a language he understands.'

'Yeah, he did tie you up and dunk you, after scaring you awake in the middle of the night,' Nish says. 'He's diabolical. An evil genius. Inua, he's giving you a run for your money.'

Inua smiles. 'I'm not saying we wage war. It's one battle. Only one. A long one. But it sends a message. One he won't forget. He'll be begging you to take him to the airport.'

Vinay is unsure. Over the next ten or so minutes, Inua lays out a plan that is so specific and well-planned and thought out: there is an equipment list, a full delegation of roles and tasks, strategies for coping with stuff that might go wrong, and a catchphrase.

'Is this a heist?' Nish says. 'I feel like we're doing a heist. Are we doing a heist?'

'We're doing a heist,' Inua says, chuckling in that high-pitched way he does when he is being a bit naughty.

'It's brilliant,' Musa says, adding the catchphrase. 'Storm the bunker.'

CHAPTER 10

Before they can start gathering things together for the heist, there is the business of the new Marvel film to go and see. It's something that has been planned for months.

Over breakfast, Vinay reads through some weathered hand-me-down comic books he

got from his cousin, trying to fill in the gaps of what might happen in Issue 3 because it's missing from the set. It's about the characters whose film they're going to see today. And Vinay loves this set of issues, because it's where the main character finds out that someone close to her is actually the hooded enemy she's been fighting this entire time, and her entire world is blown apart and she has to work out whether to try and defeat her enemy or save her friend. It is *epic*.

Vinay ignores Nikesh staring at him the entire time. All he does is slop the cereal into his mouth and hope he doesn't miss. The cinema they are going to is a short walk away, in the middle of a big estate of shops, restaurants, fun places, cars and a lonely comic book shop. They are all banned from the comic book shop because they only used to go in there to sit at the back and read, they never bought anything. Eventually, the man who works there got annoyed with them all and gave them a lifetime ban (or until one of them bought something).

None of them have been back since.

As Mum clears the bowls away and Vinay puts the cereal away, he looks at his cousin, forlorn and plan-less. He nearly falters and invites him to come, but instead just hums the Avengers theme music to himself.

'What are you doing today, Nikesh?' Mum asks Vinay's cousin.

Nikesh looks up at her and shrugs. 'Nothing,' he says. 'Same as every day. Just sit in here and watch summer go by.'

Mummy looks at Vinay and he immediately throws his hands up, like he's deflecting an energy blast from her eyes.

'No,' he says. 'No, no, no.'

'Take him,' she says. 'He'd really love it.'

'I would,' Nikesh says. 'Back home, Marvel movies were what we all used to do as a family. I miss home so much; I would love to come with you.'

'Mum, no,' Vinay says. 'We got the tickets months ago. It's going to be packed. He might not even get a ticket.'

Mummy grabs her phone and Vinay runs towards her to stop the inevitable. She scrolls around as he stands at her feet, giving her a list of reasons why Nikesh would be better off staying at home and why he and his friends deserve some time and space to themselves.

He nearly says something horrible. Something unspeakable, he's so frustrated. But he is stopped by his mum looking at him and saying, 'It's done'.

'What's done?' Vinay asks, his voice faltering. 'What's done?'

'I will go and print off the ticket for you now,' she says. 'Also, I added a popcorn for you, so get some and enjoy.'

'What?' Vinay says, outraged. His dad has banned him from eating popcorn. Apparently, Dad had a popcorn kernel stuck in between his teeth for three years and it drove him crazy and gave him gum disease and now, if anyone mentions the cinema, they have to sit through that story again. Vinay, and all his friends, know way too much about his dad's rotting gums and popcorn troubles.

When Mum is out of the room, using the printer in her bedroom, Vinay turns to Nikesh.

'You're not sitting with us,' he says.

'Why would I want to?' Nikesh replies. 'You'll just steal my popcorn.'

'I can't believe this. We've been planning

this for months.'

'Summer really isn't going your way, is it?' Nikesh says, popping an imaginary piece of popcorn into his mouth and chewing, a grin across his face, like he knows he's really nailing life.

'Nothing is,' Vinay says, getting up from the breakfast table. 'We leave at 10.'

As he walks away from the table, thinking he has made a dignified exit and can go and clean the bad taste out of his mouth with toothpaste, his mum calls to him, poking her head out of her bedroom. He spins around, saying her name in a surprised, high-pitched squeal that makes Nikesh snort.

'Aren't you going to take your bowl to the sink?' Mum asks, pointing at Vinay's discarded breakfast.

CHAPTER 11

Nikesh walks about five steps behind the council. Everyone is talking about the film, excited about what they might see. The walk to school and the walk to the cinema, which is at the end of the road their school is on, are the only times the boys get to be boys out in the world, by themselves, unsupervised, rolling in a pack, like the last gang in town.

'I hope they revisit the theme of fatherhood,' Musa says.

'I hope Hulk smashes some stuff up,' Nish says.

'In Issue 45 of World War Hulk, there is a

great scene where he battles a tank,' Inua says.

'I'm just happy to be out of the house,' Vinay says. He turns back to face Nikesh, who is scowling at them, probably annoyed by all the fan theories they're talking through. 'What about you cousin?' he asks, trying to be friendly. 'What are you most excited about?'

'The popcorn,' he says, sticking his tongue through his teeth and smirking.

'This guy,' Inua says, as Vinay turns back to carry on walking. 'Why is he with us?'

'Vinay's mum told him Nikesh has to come,' Nish says. 'It's not his choice.'

'Oh, I'm not with you guys,' Nikesh says. 'I'm just going the same way as you all, to the same place, so it's awkward that we're all walking together and I can hear every single word you're saying.'

'You could cross the road, man,' Inua says.

'It's shady on this side,' Nikesh says.

They keep walking and arguing and, without thinking, Nish starts to walk onto a zebra crossing, as if they're going to school.

'Wrong way, Nish!' Musa shouts.

A car screeches to a halt at the zebra crossing, just as Nish steps back on to the pavement, throwing out a big doofus roll of his eyes at himself. Everyone laughs.

Suddenly, a car door slams open, and a man jumps out of the car, crossing around and pointing at Nish.

'What do you think you're doing?' he screams. 'I stopped for you. You said you were going to cross the road. Cross the road, now. I have stopped for you.'

Nish looks around, confused, as if to say, *what on earth is going on?*

'Sorry,' he says. 'My mistake. Carry on.'

'Carry on?' the man shouts, like the gang

has shut his foot in a bear trap AND put a melting ice-cream just out of his reach. 'I stopped for you. I stopped my entire day for you to cross the road, and now you don't want to cross the road. You young people, you children, you think the whole world just revolves around you. And it doesn't, okay?!'

'Dude,' Inua says. 'It wasn't that bad, was it? Less than a minute of a delay.'

'Mistakes happen,' Musa adds.

'Leave our friend alone,' Vinay says.

'You are taking this way too seriously,' Nish says, cackling. 'Which is a ridiculous thing for me to say.'

The cackling seems to do something to the car driver because he suddenly runs forward, his hands flailing. The crew don't quite know what to do, or what has triggered this utterly over-the-top response to such a small thing. Nish screams, Inua starts edging backwards, Musa holds his group, Vinay grabs Nish's hand.

'Get back in the car,' they all hear, assertive and commanding. 'Now.'

The man stops running; a blockade has emerged between him and the group of cowering friends.

'What is this?' he says.

Vinay looks, his friends look, and there stands Nikesh, holding a hand up to the car driver, as if to say *no, you do not do this.*

'Get back in the car and drive away now, and I won't tell anyone you nearly tried to attack these people.'

'Who are you?' the driver asks, his voice almost muffled by the beeping drivers wanting him to get back in his car and move it.

'I'm the guy telling you that you need to get in your car, and drive away. I have recorded your licence plate number. And need I remind you that assaulting children is a crime, and you could be arrested.'

This is enough to make the driver drop his hands by his side and think for a second.

Looking at the council of pals, and with the ringing and ringing of car horns all around him, he realises he is losing a battle. Nikesh stands his ground and puts his hand on his hips. As the car driver walks away, embarrassed now, he shouts at the kids to *watch themselves* and *be careful* and how they were *lucky this time*. He drives off and the boys stand there.

They all stare at Nikesh.

Vinay approaches him.

'That was incredible,' he says. 'You were so clear with him. And he did what you said.'

'You guys need to take care of yourselves better. Otherwise, you really will run into trouble,' Nikesh says. 'Don't be cowards all your life.'

★★★

That comment from Nikesh really hurts Vinay and stays with him all the way through the film. He doesn't really concentrate. He's lost in his thoughts, arguing with Nikesh in his head about how strong he is, how wrong Nikesh is, how he would have handled the whole situation had Nikesh not intervened, how Nikesh needs to be nicer to him and his friends (and could he share his popcorn?).

Nikesh sits rows in front of them, directly in Vinay's of line of sigh, and his laughter penetrates the busy cinema. The rustling of his popcorn is louder than the bangs and smacks and explosions and fighting on the screen. Vinay cannot concentrate on the film at all.

And, when they all walk home, talking about what an amazing film it was, Nikesh is amongst them all, agreeing and disagreeing with opinions and reminding people of cool lines and big fun stunts that they all start acting out. And Vinay is five steps behind. Walking by himself. Watching his cousin steal his friends right out from under him. Especially Nish, who is laughing the hardest and the loudest: his first ever friend.

Vinay remembers the first time he spoke to Nish. It was the second day of school, and he was still so nervous about being new. Everybody else would know each other from Year 1 and potentially even Reception. But he was new to the dynamic, so how on earth was he going to fit into the class? His first day, he hadn't spoken to anyone at all. It had been so lonely.

He arrived early on the second day. Before

everyone else, and, because he was new and didn't need to hang about in the playground until it was time to go to his class, he found himself in his classroom waiting for his teacher and classmates to arrive. The classroom was blank. It was the start of term, and the empty walls invited the coming year's work to fill it. He took out his notebook. He was trying to teach himself to draw Spidey; he had such good ideas for a Spider-Man storyline that he drew all these stick figure Spideys, all in action, jumping, crawling, punching, thwipping, before adding in the contours of actual bodies when he had the stick angles right. He couldn't draw as well as Inua, he would later find out, but Inua would show him how to visualise images before drawing them as triangles. He was drawing the head, puzzling over the best way to emphasis the head of the villain Hammerhead, when he saw the door open and in walk a pupil who was short and had big curly hair that added a few inches to his height. He wore a Nike headband around his hair and headphones. He sat down next to Vinay and smiled.

'Hey,' he said. 'I'm Nish. I'm left-handed too.'

'One in ten people,' Vinay replied, not knowing what else to say.

'And there's twenty people in the class. And you and I . . . we're the chosen ones. The lefties. I guess we should sit together and become best friends and form a club where if anyone ever wrongs us, the other will seek retribution.'

'I'm in,' Vinay replied, smiling at the incredibly warm welcome. 'I'm Vinay by the way.'

'What are you drawing? Is that Hammerhead?' Nish asked, pushing his head closer to the paper for a better look. 'The Spidey villain?'

Vinay nodded, unsure of how gassed to be or not. He knew that this wasn't exactly what the cool kids sat around and chatted about if they wanted to make a good impression in new places. There was football and music and LEGO to discuss, people to make fun of, and teachers to snark about. But maybe being honest about this very specific love of his life could result in a best friend.

'He has a much rounder head, I reckon. Not as square,' Nish said. He picked up a pencil and drew what he meant. It was perfect. It worked. Vinay smiled.

'I'm so glad you don't think this isn't stupid,' he said, smiling.

'Of course it isn't. I love Spidey. He is the coolest superhero. Of all of them. I've never seen anyone try to draw him.'

'I want to make my own comics.'

'That's funny,' Nish said. 'I want to be a comic when I'm older.'

'Tell jokes?'

'Yeah bebe,' Nish said, and Vinay laughed.

'Now we've formed a club,' Nish said. 'You have to meet my boy Musa. He'd be into this too.'

And that was all it took. Sometimes, that is all it takes to meet new best friends. Sometimes all it takes is just finding that you like the same things.

★★★

As Nish laughs, Vinay tells him to not wet himself. Nish stops in his tracks. He stares at his friend like he has cut him deep.

'We don't talk about that,' he says, furiously.

'Don't talk about what?' Inua asks.

'Yeah, don't talk about what?' Musa says, before noting Nish's reaction and grimacing, like he's made a mistake.

'Nothing,' Nish says, exploding, talking really fast, like he does when he is stressed. 'I had an accident, okay? We went out to the movies, and you know my rule, I don't leave the movie 'til it's finished. They don't put ad breaks in movies for a reason. And it was a hot day and I had drunk a lot of water, cos as Musa says . . .'

'Stay hydrated,' everyone choruses.

'Exactly, stay hydrated. I did. And I had an accident. And Vin here told me to just go to the loo, and I didn't because, well, you know, what if I missed something important or obscured the view for someone else, and look, I can hold in a wee, I'm not two.'

'He didn't hold in the wee,' Vinay says, snorting, laughing, before seeing the absolute pain and embarrassment on Nish's face and quieting himself.

Nikesh bursts into laughter, pointing at Nish, falling over himself, leaning, hands on knees, wheezing, his high-pitched shriek breaking into coughs, his laughter ringing around the busy, bustling town centre.

'You guys are so funny, dude,' he says, thought his coughing. 'You all act like you're these super cool, better than everyone grown-ups, but you're all just babies. Waaah, waaah, I can't do wee-wees in the toilet. Waaah, waaah, he took my bed, mummy, mummy, solve my problems.'

Nish looks at Vinay with utter disgust. Vinay understands that he has wronged his friend. After the accident, Nish hid in the toilets and Vinay ran to the nearest cheap clothes shop and used up all their pooled money to buy the cheapest thing in there that was Nish's size; which was a bright lime green pair of cycling shorts that were made to be seen by drivers, so they were definitely going to be seen by every pedestrian around. Vinay ran back to the cinema to find Nish standing outside, crying, his trousers a state.

'They found me and chucked me out,' he said. 'They said I was trying to sneak into another screening.'

'Oh man,' Vinay said.

'What did you get me?' Nish asked.

Vinay showed him the bicycle shorts and Nish burst into tears out of frustration. Vinay couldn't even comfort him with a cuddle because of, well, the accident.

★★★

That night, lying in bed, Vinay stares at the bottom of the top bunk. Inua and Musa took Nish home, as furious as he was with Vinay. And Vinay and Nikesh went home together in silence. Over dinner, as they ate dal bhatt shaak rotli, Mum was very complimentary to Dad about Vinay looking after his cousin. Dad didn't even look away from the cricket as he offered his son a well done.

When Jadeja scored a six, he screamed a *ya ya ya ya* at an extremely high pitch. Nikesh stood up from the table and celebrated with him and they danced around the room, arms linked like they are at a wedding doing some ballroom moves. Vinay watched and felt increasingly like he was losing his place in the world.

Now, he lies there listening to Nikesh's snoring and feeling angry that he has lost so much today. And on a Marvel movie day. Twice a year, sometimes three, he gets to celebrate the gloriousness of his favourite characters on screen. Today feels different somehow.

Vinay has one of those nights where his sleep is fitful and he doesn't feel like he's getting any rest, but he has lots of dreams, all of them about being alone. Nikesh snores through the night, which makes Vinay angry.

He realises that he needs to do something to take back control. It's the only way. This realisation finally sends him to sleep.

CHAPTER 12

The next morning, Vinay sleeps in late, having struggled to quiet his mind enough to get some rest. He wakes to a familiar laugh. Springing out of bed, he runs towards Musa's warmth, throwing open the door, welcoming the day and stepping into . . .

A breakfast scene he has not anticipated. Musa and Nikesh: eating toast and laughing.

It takes Vinay a second to catch up with what they're saying, but they're both talking about last year's World Cup final, and the thrilling penalty shootout that ended things for the team they both love.

Vinay looks at Musa like *what on earth are you doing?* and Musa offers a thumbs up to him.

'Go get ready,' Musa says. 'Big day. It's okay. Your cousin can keep me company.'

He smiles at Vinay like everything is fine, but everything is definitely not fine. *How dare he side with Nikesh and be friends with him after all he has done?* Vinay thinks.

Vinay has lost another one of his council.

Furious, he heads back to his room to change. He gets ready, brushes his teeth and runs past Musa and Nikesh, eating and laughing, straight out of the door, heading for Vinville, a secret place only he knows.

Vinville is Vinay's alone place. Each of the council has one, located in close proximity around their estate. Vin's is a shed that is rotting away, on a piece of allotment land that has been abandoned. It's completely empty. No one uses the allotment, let alone the shed, and it is overgrown with long grass and unexpected berries that provide bowls and bowls of fresh fruit for Nish's mum to make into jam for everyone.

He keeps the shed empty, in case anyone ever claims it and he finds his stuff gone, or the shed demolished. It is already falling down around him.

Here, he sits and stares at the plastic window, bubbling in the heat. You can't see in or out anymore, because of the warped material, but also because of the decades of grim and moss and dirt that have smeared it. Here, he can truly feel alone and be in his feelings.

He considers everything that has happened. The arrival of his cousin has caused him to lose his bedroom, his bunk bed and now two of his friends. Musa, of all people, understands loyalty, surely. And Nish, the guy who was his first real friend. He remembers Musa telling him about the first day he'd joined school. The pain it held for him.

How he was introduced by his status and then his name, and he watched as a sea of smiling faces made decisions about him. Their faces looked like pity. And there was that one kid, Nish, who just shouted 'oo-ooooo' like he already knew he was a fan of that song, and he'd felt immediately in his care. Nish stood up and high-fived him and it was like everyone else breathed a sigh of relief that he was taken care of. He never wanted to feel like a burden to anyone. Especially not to Nish, but Nish's joy was really that he was into you being you. And when Nish introduced him to Vinay and he saw that Vinay was single-minded and determined and also supportive, he knew he had friends for life.

His sister always told him, when he missed their mother and father, when they were on their big journey, that 'they are in your heart'. She reminded him that the last time he saw them, as though they both knew it would be a long time before they were able to reconnect, his mother bent down and kissed them both and she rubbed their cheeks back and forth vigorously.

'There, so it can last a while,' she said, as she stood up to leave.

'I'm going to miss you,' Musa told her.

She smiled, sweetly, and said, 'That's why I rubbed the kisses in. So they can go into your bloodstream and pump around your heart. That way I'm always with you. But listen, family is about the ones we choose as well, okay.'

Family is about the ones we choose, Vinay thinks, *as well as the ones we are related to.* Vinay decides to fight for his chosen family. He stands up and leaves Vinville, running in the direction of the council den.

CHAPTER 13

Vinay arrives at the tree to find it empty. It's the summer holidays and they are always here. Without fail. To see it empty, to be the first one here, even when Inua's mum, who works at the hospital, leaves so early that he is up and ready for action way before anyone else is awake, is a strange feeling.

He's never the first one here. He pulls himself up on to the platform to see if a note has been left for him.

Absolutely nothing.

He jumps back down and looks around him, listening for the whistle in the trees to see if he can hear any voices. It's the summer holidays. This is the meeting spot. It's strange that none of them are here.

He decides to go into Inua's flat to see why he hasn't come out into his garden yet. Inua hasn't betrayed him yet. Inua's twin, who Musa calls Twinua, even though her name is Yasmeen, says she hasn't seen him all morning, while her dad, fresh from a night shift, shouts for a tea and to close the door because it was making the house cold and drafty. This makes Vinay smile. Classic immigrant parents, just like his, always cold, even during a heatwave, like the midday sun is nothing at all compared to where they grew up.

Vinay goes to Nish's house and his mum answers the door. He is still embarrassed because of how he talked to Nish yesterday, betraying his trust. When Nish's mum answers the door, she is very surprised to see him. She has a black apron on, caked with flour, and a rolling pin in her hand. She takes one look at Vinay and says, 'Not here,' loudly and clearly, then closes the door in his face.

Vinay starts walking across the courtyard of the estate, towards the block where he and Musa live. Musa's probably playing cards in his room with his cousin or something. Musa can be like that sometimes. He can try and bring peace in the biggest way possible, by trying to bring everyone together. It sometimes means they don't always talk about what's annoyed them. Usually, it takes Vinay to get everyone to clear the air. That's why they all work so well as a team: Inua has the blue-sky thinking, Nish keeps everyone going and has a good sense of humour about him, Musa tries to see all angles and bring peace, and Vinay makes everyone be honest. It's a great dynamic. It's a shame that Nikesh has come in and ruined it with his presence, his chaos, his meanness.

As Vinay crosses the courtyard, he can hear Musa's laugh echoing all around him, like it's taunting him. He looks around trying to source it, running towards the grassy verge where they sometimes play football.

What he stumbles upon is surprising. Nish is batting. Nikesh is bowling. Musa and Inua sit and watch.

'What is going on here?' Vinay asks, sadly, feeling even more left out.

Inua turns to him and shakes his head. Right then, Nikesh bowls and Nish goes for a whacker, trying to lift the ball over their building or something, but the shot is mistimed. He swings way too early, and the tennis ball sails under, past him and demolishes the stumps. Nikesh celebrates with the loudest *howszaaaat* known to man, shrieked loud enough to shatter windows.

Nish throws his bat on the floor.

'Why did you distract me?' he shouts, as Nikesh picks the bat up and runs to fetch the ball from where it has bounced under a car.

'Sorry man,' Vinay says. 'What's going on here?'

'I'm showing your friends a real sport,' Nikesh shouts across. 'They keep talking about basketball and football. Cricket is a real sport, a god's sport.'

'A coloniser's sport,' Inua mutters and Musa laughs.

'I like cricket,' Vinay says.

'Do you?' Nikesh says, thumping at the ground with his bat. 'I thought it might be too brainy for you.'

'I'm brainy,' Vinay says, defiantly. 'Bit mean.'

'I just mean, cricket is like chess and baseball, all at the same time. It's not always about staying in and hitting boundaries, and it's not all about bouncers and googlies. It's about knowing when best to play them.'

'No wonder each match lasts five days,' Musa says, looking at Inua.

'I'm surprised the colonisers had so much time on their hands. Weren't they busy colonising?'

Nish laughs. He takes a run up and delivers a mid-paced ball that Nikesh isn't quite ready for. As a result, he mistimes his stroke, and the odd tuft of grass throws the ball up into bat. It's a tennis ball, so tends to bounce off any hard surface. It goes flying into the air.

Feeling like a hero who can show his friends, nah, his best friends, just who he is, Vinay runs forward, jumping over Musa and Inua, as the ball flies high into the air, and Nikesh shouts *noooooooooo* and Nish shouts *yesssss*. Vinay, feeling like everything moves into slow-motion, jumps forward, his arms stretched, his hands together and cupped in front of him, as he dives forward, forward, forward and the ball, dropping down from its impossible, high arc, plops into his hands, like there is no question, no deniability. Nikesh is out.

Nish screams, *howzaaaaaaat*, so loudly that

someone opens a window in their building and shushes him, and he shouts sorry, just as loudly, which leads someone else to shush him for apologising for the shush, and so on; he is caught in a shush-apology tour. Meanwhile, Nikesh throws his bat on the floor and turns to Vinay.

'Why were you distracting me?' he shouts.

He walks off in the direction of the apartment building. He turns back to Vinay and his friends and shouts, 'I am going to make your life miserable.'

Inua applauds, saluting Vinay. Nish walks over to him.

'I think you should go and talk to him,' Nish says. 'He seems pretty upset.'

'Why are you siding with him?' Vinay says, jabbing a finger in Nish's chest. 'In fact,' he adds, turning to Musa, 'why were you having breakfast and laughing with him?

You're supposed to be my friends.'

'Of course we're your friends,' Musa says. 'I was trying to help you. I wanted to try and find out more about him.'

'And I was just being nice to him because he's part of our lives now,' Nish adds. 'Are we supposed to be mean to the guy who you share a bedroom with forever?'

'It's a betrayal,' Vinay says, pointing at Inua. 'Inua is the only one who understands. Inua, it's time.'

Inua jumps to his feet.

'Oh hell yes,' he says. 'I'm gonna run home. We need more buckets for what I have planned.'

'I don't think this is such a good idea,' Musa says.

'It's too late,' Vinay replies, running after Inua. 'Let the chaos reign.'

CHAPTER 14

Nish and Musa get involved, much to their annoyance, much to their grumbling. They make peace with Nikesh and take him back outside, so he is distracted while Inua and Vinay rig the bedroom up. Buckets of water, poured out on to Nikesh's mattress, to make it sopping. They take a plastic 'red alert' button Inua got given for Christmas: every time you press it, a big alarm sounds, and a robot voice barks *red alert red alert*. They put it inside Nikesh's pillow case. It's such a sensitive button, and so unnecessarily loud.

They set up a few other booby traps and, as Inua finishes up, Vinay takes his Arsenal poster and his Spider-Man poster from the top of the wardrobe, where they've been lying flat under a bunch of books, and he attaches them to the wall with some tack, careful to ensure they are straight, prominent and the first things he sees when he wakes up. He lies on his bed and looks at them from the vantage point of his pillow.

He stands up and high-fives Inua, who is climbing down the ladder.

'Are you ready for what comes next?' Inua asks. 'Because you cannot undo this. When elephants fight, it's the grass that suffers. I will help you because I believe that sometimes the best way to stand up to someone is to take control of the fight. But at the same time, I need you to understand that this is it. You do not come back from this. Are you prepared for what happens next?'

Vinay nods. He is furious, and he cannot think straight, but he knows that the only way this interloper in his life is going to learn is through a show of force.

'I am,' he says.

He high-fives his poster of Spidey on his way out. Inua watches him, shaking his head, unsure that this is how Peter Parker would go about solving his problems. He would probably just talk to the guy.

Vinay sees his mum in the kitchen, making a big batch of rotlis for when the baby comes. She is stocking up the freezer. Vinay asks if she needs any help, and she quickly involves him and Inua into the assembly line.

She stands at the stove and cooks the rotlis. Inua pinches out balls of dough from the motherlode and rolls them into balls, before flattening them in the palm of his hands and pulling them out into circles. Vinay, kneeling on Ba's stool, rolls the discs out with the rolling pin, 'til they fill the circumference of the board in front of him. Mum then grabs them and puts them on to the tawa.

Eventually, there is a knock at the door, and Inua, having reduced the mother dough to individual balls and now rinsing out the glass bowl at the sink, goes to open it.

It's Nish and Musa, both looking angry and dishevelled. There is mud on Nish's face and Musa has a torn t-shirt.

'What happened?' Inua asks.

'Ask his cousin,' Musa mumbles.

'Who's hungry?' Mum asks.

As the boys sit around the table eating hot rotlis smeared with chocolate spread, Mum circles the table, before settling behind her favourite, Musa, and putting her hands on his shoulders and smiling at her son and his best friends.

'Where is your cousin?' she asks. 'In his room?'

'The less said about that man the better,' Musa says, chewing a mouthful of rotli, a teardrop of chocolate drooping from his

118

bottom lip, which he licks away.

'Where is he?'

'We left him outside, practising his bowling against the back of the garages,' Nish says. 'He seemed happy.'

'Vinay,' Mum shouts, plonking herself down at the table. 'This isn't good enough. He is your cousin. He is your responsibility. He is family. Don't let him play by himself.'

'He isn't the easiest . . .' Nish starts to say, but Vinay coughs over him.

Vinay has tried this before and that made his mum even angrier, saying, *why couldn't he find something they both liked?*

'Vinay,' Mum says. 'I'm disappointed in you.'

'I didn't ask for him to move in, did I? No one asked me,' Vinay shouts, standing up from the table and running to the bathroom.

Once he has calmed down, and his friends have told him he has to apologise to his mum, Vinay does so.

He knocks on her bedroom door and waits for her to say, sleepily, for him to come in. He hovers by the door.

'Sorry,' he says, as quickly as he can, not fully convinced by his own apology.

'Come in, darling,' he hears his mum say. 'Come and give me a hug.'

'Give her a hug,' Nish whispers from the doorway.

'Hi Nish,' Mum says.

'Hi auntie,' Nish replies.

Vinay grimaces at his friends and shuts the door in their faces. He walks over to the bed where his mum is sleeping with a cushion between her legs,

on her side, facing the window, where the curtains bulge and billow with the summer breeze.

'What do you have to say to me?'

'I'm sorry.'

'What for?'

'What do you mean?'

'Darling,' Mum says, opening her eyes. 'You have to know what you're saying sorry for. Otherwise, it's pointless.'

'Oh,' Vinay says. 'I'm sorry for disappointing you. I think that's it. I think I am sorry for disappointing you.'

'You think you are sorry for disappointing me?' Mum says. 'Is that really it?'

'I don't know,' Vinay says, welling up into tears.

Vinay runs into the corner of the room and stands facing the wall.

'What's wrong darling?'

'I do everything wrong,' he says, through tears, conscious that there is an audience on the other side of the door. He is really upset though and can't stop the tears from coming, and the embarrassment he feels from reacting this way, when this was not the plan, the embarrassment he feels that his friends can hear him cry, his embarrassment that he prepared himself to give his mother an apology and she won't accept it because it's for the wrong thing. All of it is a cloud over him, raining, raining, raining down his face.

'Darling,' Mum says. 'Come here.'

He shakes his head.

She says it again, more firmly, reminding him that it's harder for her to move than it is for him.

Vinay lies down next to his mum and cuddles her.

'If this is about the bedroom, I don't

want to hear it,' she says. 'For as long as he wants to, your cousin is living with us and that's final.'

'I know,' Vinay says, trying to calm himself. Then it hits him. The important words in his mum's sentence. For as long as he wants to . . .

Vinay springs out of bed and runs to the door.

'That it?' his mum says. 'I don't think we solved anything.'

'I'm fine,' he replies, not really listening to what she is saying.

He opens the door.

'Hostile environment it is,' he whispers to his friends, which makes Inua break out into a huge smile.

'Yeah, I'm not sure I like this,' Musa replies.

Inua arrived into their lives as chaotically as he exists in it. He threw a basketball to Vinay as he, Musa and Nish left for school one day. Vinay caught the basketball and looked around to see who it belonged to. That's when Inua came bounding up to him, smiling and shouting 'nice catch'.

He walked to school with them all, slotting into the conversation perfectly and without question, and hung out with them at school, and talked and talked, and asked questions and told stories about animals that were actually metaphors for life. And before they all knew it, they had a new member of the gang. And it was like he had been there the whole time. He had joined school a term in and that had given him a little bit of anxiety about making friends, but when he saw the crew, and overheard them talking about Star

Wars Rebels the first week of school, he knew he had found his people.

★★★

Inua tests the rest of the equipment while Vinay, Nish and Musa all keep Nikesh talking on the sofa. Inua emerges, winks at everyone and he, Musa and Nish head back to their houses for the evening, leaving Vinay and Nikesh sitting on the sofa in silence.

Nikesh yawns.

'I'm tired,' he says. 'Time for me to head to my room to go to sleep on my bunk bed. Good night.'

'You not having dinner?' Vinay asks.

'No, I'm tired.'

Vinay feels a flutter of excitement inside him. This is it now. The homestretch. He decides to go to bed too, just to watch.

Revenge, sweet revenge: it approaches, and it has Vinay's beaming face all over it.

★★★

As Nikesh does what he needs to in the bathroom, Vinay lies on his bed, noticing a few drops of water have sopped onto his bed and a trail of dangerous condensation from the heat in the room has created a halo all around his bedframe.

Nikesh enters the room, pulls his socks off and makes a fart noise in Vinay's direction. Vinay just smiles and closes his eyes. It does not bother him. He is about to get exactly what he has been waiting for. His own room. Because tonight, Nikesh is going to find out exactly what happens when you cross a man like Vinay.

Nikesh starts climbing up the ladder in his bare feet, but he slips and slams his shins into the frame, crying out in pain. Inua and Vinay laced the ladder with slime they made, using jelly and jam mixed together. Nikesh grumbles and fumbles and makes his way to the top, making small noises about his ouchy shins.

Vinay hears him flop onto the bed with a slam. The waft sends the halo of water droplets cascading around Vinay, like he's in a film and the rain is falling in slow motion.

Vinay stifles a giggle as he feels Nikesh shuffle up the bed and slam his head into the pillow.

ERRRRR ERRRR ERRRR RED ALERT

Nikesh hears, and he shouts out in surprise, shocked at the noise. Vinay tries not to laugh, issuing a snoring noise, so it appears he is asleep.

Nikesh pulls open the covers of the bed and settles in.

It must be soaking because Nikesh says, 'What on earth? Why is it so wet?'

Vinay has to keep doing his snoring noise. He wants to laugh so badly. Because this is only getting started.

Nikesh lies back down on his pillow to the sound of **ERRRRR ERRRR ERRRR RED ALERT**, and as he shifts about, trying to get comfortable, Vinay reaches out with his foot and kicks at the broom at the bottom of his bed. He sleeps the opposite way to Nikesh, so his feet are where Nikesh's pillow is, and the broom prods at a bucket, resting on the edge of the bedframe, which tumbles, splash, all over Nikesh, dousing him, starting him to stand up, where he bangs his head on the ceiling, falling back down on to the pillow and **ERRRRR ERRRR ERRRR RED ALERT ERRRRR ERRRR ERRRR RED ALERT ERRRRR ERRRR ERRRR RED ALERT**.

He is grumbling, grumbling and **ERRRRR ERRRR ERRRR RED ALERT** and he screams in frustration and Vinay cannot help himself, he lets out a giggle, asking if Nikesh is okay, through the darkness, his voice filled with giggles and giggles.

'You,' Nikesh shouts. 'It's you.'

He is thundering across the bed. He puts his hands on the ladder, in the darkness, and the slimy jam-jelly concoction makes his hands slip, and he stumbles as he judders down the bunk bed, shaking the entire frame.

'You,' Nikesh keeps shouting, angrier, and angrier, making Vinay nervous he's going to wake someone up. The television is on in the next room. Mum and Dad are probably up watching one of their shows.

As Nikesh reaches the ground, he steps into the piece de resistance: a bucket of icy water, which makes him yelp, and jump, straight into a second bucket, of warm water, before he trips and crashes to the floor with a splash and a bang and a thud and a groan. The water gushes across the floor.

Vinay is on his feet, immediately, switching the light on, and standing over his cousin.

'This is my room,' he shouts. 'You are a guest in here. Now, whose room is this?'

Nikesh looks up at Vinay, and whimpers, his face crumbling, his lips quivering and finally, although he tries to hold it in as long as he can, he bursts into tears. Loud, wailing tears.

'I want to go home,' he shouts. 'I want to go home.'

Vinay laughs at his cousin, but as his cries get more uncontrollable, Vinay starts to realise that something has happened here, and as Musa said, there was no going back from this.

The door bursts open, and Mum and Dad are standing in the doorway.

'What on earth?' his dad shouts, angrily. 'Did you do this?'

He points at Vinay and Vinay nods, now crying too.

Both him and his cousin, crying, look at each other, and in that moment, Vinay doesn't see an enemy, he sees one of his own, upset by his actions. And this makes him sit down on the cold, wet carpet, and cry into the palms of his hands.

'Nikesh, beta,' Mum says. 'Come and

sleep in our bedroom. Vinay will get this all cleaned up.'

Nikesh stands up and accepts a hug from Vinay's mum. Vinay's dad throws a stack of towels at Vinay, telling him to dry the carpets.

CHAPTER 15

The morning comes and Vinay emerges from the bedroom, which smells like a wet dog. It is quiet in the flat. Mum sits on the sofa in front of the news, eating grapes. She looks at him and then back at the television. The table is empty.

'Where is everybody?'

'Your father is at work,' Mum says.

'And my cousin?'

'He wanted to walk around the neighbourhood one last time. Then he and I will look at flight times and get him back home. Which everyone is not very happy about. But he thinks it will be better for him than the welcome he has received here.'

'Sorry,' Vinay says.

'Do you know what you are apologising for?'

'Not making an effort with him,' Vinay says, his head bowed, his cheeks burning with guilt.

'I think you should find him,' Mum says.

★★★

Vinay gets changed in record time, grabbing a banana for the road. His first stop is Nish's flat. Nish is sitting on the stairs outside his door, playing on his Switch.

'Come with me,' Vinay says.

'Where are we going?'

'Just come.'

Vinay grabs Musa, then Inua, and then his gang runs around the estate, looking for

Nikesh, before heading to Inua's to the den.

Everyone is silent. Mostly because Vinay is silent, and they are feeding off the energy emanating from him.

Vinay spies Nikesh in Inua's back garden, holding a big stick, whacking it against a tree in frustration.

'Nikesh!' Vinay shouts.

Nikesh, hearing his name and seeing who is calling for him, drops the stick in fear, and runs.

'No!' Vinay shouts. 'We come in peace!'

He breaks into a run after his cousin, through the garden, weaving in between the thick hedges, jumping over fallen branches and sidestepping erratic paving slabs.

Nikesh runs with one eye on his shoulder and so doesn't see when a low-lying branch clotheslines him and sends him crashing to the floor.

Vinay reaches him, panting, and his three best friends approach.

'Come to finish the job?' Nikesh says. 'Don't worry. I am leaving. My ba will look after me.'

'No,' Vinay says. 'Look, come with us. I want to talk to you, in front of all of you. I have some things to say.'

★★★

The council den is filled with a quiet sense of doom. There is a thick cloud hanging over Vinay as he leads the way.

Nikesh walks in between him and the other three boys.

Inua tries to break the silence by talking about his summer plans and a trip to a swimming pool he has heard the love of his life, Simran, goes to.

'Maybe we should go,' he says. 'We can

swim, play some sports, and just hang out.'

'Sounds good,' Musa says. 'All that nourishing Vitamin D. Inject it into my veins.'

'Will Simran be there?' Nish asks and they all laugh.

'Who's Simran?' Nikesh adds, and Vinay turns to him.

'Someone Inua has been in love with since the first day of school.'

'Look, guys, that's just not true. She's just a friend that I want to spend all my time with.'

Nikesh laughs, understanding, and for the first time in this visit, Vinay sees his cousin's face. Gone is the scowl, gone is the anger, gone is the arrogant front. Instead, this person laughing here and now, this is his cousin.

They arrive at the council's den and

Vinay leads the way up on to the platform, followed by Nikesh and then his friends. They all sit in a circle and Vinay clears his throat, nervous about what's going to happen.

CHAPTER 16

'Thanks everyone for coming,' Vinay says. 'All I wanted was a council of good friends, each one with our different skills and interests. And I have one, and Nikesh, I think you would benefit from a council as well. You seem like you need a good group of friends around you. And I don't want to hog all the best people. For you, or for Simran.'

Inua snorts.

Musa nods proudly.

Nish fails to sit still because cross-legged is way more difficult than it looks.

'I don't understand,' Nikesh says.

'I should have asked you this a while ago, and I'm sorry I didn't. I'm sorry to you, and I'm sorry to Nish, who suggested it in the first place. But I need to ask, are you okay?'

The thing about someone looking you in the eye and asking if you are okay is it seems like the simplest question in the world, and we ask it all the time, but rarely does the situation mean we get an honest answer. It's just something we do: *Hey how are you? Fine how are you?*

Sometimes, though, asking someone how they are, and if they're ok, and showing them you really care about their answer, so they can be as truthful as they want to be, it can be the most human thing you can do in your life.

'No,' Nikesh says, and he cries.

It takes him a few minutes to collect himself, because he tries to speak through the tears and he can't, and then he gets frustrated with himself for not being able to say what he's thinking or stop crying. Vinay offers him a hug and he accepts it, which surprises Vin, so he squeezes tight. Nish and Inua join in and finally Musa, thundering some pats across everyone's backs.

From within the melee of cuddle, comes a little voice, slowly pulling itself together, 'I'm okay, I'm okay,' and slowly the friends break and sit back down, all except Nish, who stands.

'Sorry to hear that, Nikesh,' Vinay says. 'Want to talk about it?'

'I'm so far away from home,' Nikesh says. 'And I miss my home. I miss my dad and I'm sad that he is having to work so much to earn money to move here, and I miss Mum every single day. I really miss her. She just isn't there anymore. And I know that Dad is doing what he needs to do to ensure I am near my family. But it's hard. None of this is what I know. This isn't my home.'

'It is,' Vinay says. 'For as long as you live with us, it is your home.'

'I think that's why I was so adamant it was my room and my bunk bed. It could be my fortress . . .'

'Like Superman?' Inua asks. 'Like his Fortress of Solitude?'

'Exactly,' says Nikesh. 'I've never had my own room before. And I got excited. And I was mad at being sent away even though I know it was the right thing, and it is really nice of Auntie and you and Uncle and Ba to open your house to me . . .'

'Of course, you're family.'

'I was sad, and I took it out on you.'

'I could have acted nicer,' Vinay says. 'I've never had my own room either. And it just became a big important thing in my head. And actually, the more important thing was, I was growing my family. And I should have thought about that.'

'I'm sorry,' Nikesh says. 'You guys are cool. Thank you.'

'I forgive you,' Vinay says. 'And I'm sorry too.'

'I'm not sorry,' Inua says. 'The traps I set you were magnificent.'

'And I'm sorry I didn't force Vin to ask you how you were earlier,' Nish says. 'I knew it was the right thing.'

'And I'm sorry that I look so fresh this morning,' Musa says. And they laugh, all together. Before him, Vinay regards the council, his council, now with one more person.

'So,' Inua asks. 'If you're joining the council, what are you bringing to the table?'

Nikesh thinks about it. 'Vibes.'

They laugh again.

★★★

As Musa, Inua and Nish jump around the garden, Vinay and Nikesh sit on the pallet and talk.

'How are we going to make this work?'

Nikesh asks. 'You and me. Because your mum is about to have a baby, we can't really bring more chaos into the house.'

'We just need to make sure that if we annoy each other, because we probably will, we sort it out amongst ourselves. We cannot let it get to Inua wetting up the entire place levels of chaos.'

'True, although that room does get quite hot, so it might be needed.'

'Very true. I think if we have a disagreement that we can't sort between us, we have our boys.'

Nikesh looks at his hands and starts shaking again, he is crying.

'What did I say?' Vinay asks.

'Our boys,' Nikesh replies. 'I've not had many friends in my life.'

Vinay smiles and stands up, offering a hand to Nikesh.

They climb down the tree and stand in the garden. The rest of the boys stop what they're doing and gather around them.

'Boys, we are a council now, with Nikesh a fully paid-up member. We have some systems to work through, so we don't all fall out and invoke the Inua Chaos Protocol, but we're going to be fine. I believe in us.'

Vinay holds out his hand and everyone clasps it.

CHAPTER 17

You can hear them before you see them, thundering through the courtyard at full gallop: Vinay leading the pack, giggling like a terrified chicken, Musa running fast and focused, and Inua, leaping as if he hopes each stride will bring him closer to take off (one day, he will learn to fly). Nikesh is stumbling, miscalculating the speed with which Nish operates when there is mischief to be had. They're being chased by Nish, wielding two large canons, each one attached to a canister of coloured water: one purple, one orange. He sprays water after them.

This time Vinay is prepared, jumping behind a tree and scrambling to the spot where he'd hidden some contraband earlier.

Reaching down, he finds four more canons, all red, and all filled with red water. He grabs them and throws them to Musa, Inua and Nikesh, holding one back for himself.

'Mutually assured destruction,' Musa shouts, as they all stand in a circle pointing their canons at each other.

'I . . . did not plan for this,' Nish says, looking down at the Man U top he wears with such pride. 'Wait.'

He drops his canon, pulls the top off revealing his white undershirt, as he throws his pride and joy safely to one side.

Vinay smiles, shouting, 'one, two, three' and the canons all hit their targets, and all you can hear, on this still, hot summer's day is the sound of five boys, laughing and laughing and laughing, not just because they have each other, but because that water is really cold (Vinay froze the canons overnight, and let them melt in the sun).

Just another day for the council of good friends.

ACKNOWLEDGEMENTS

Thanks to the entire Knights Of team, especially Eishar Brar and Aimée Felone. Thank you to Dee Stevens. To Rochelle Falconer. To my agent Julia Kingsford. To Nerm, Nikita Gill and Anoushka Shankar. To Chimene Suleyman. To Gavin James Bower. To my family. And to my own Council Of Good Friends: Musa Okwonga, Nish Kumar, Vinay Patel and Inua Ellams. To Rob. And to Steelo Brown.

NIKESH SHUKLA

Author

Nikesh Shukla is a novelist and screenwriter. He is the author of *Coconut Unlimited* (shortlisted for the Costa First Novel Award), *Meatspace* and the critically acclaimed *The One Who Wrote Destiny*. Nikesh is the editor of the bestselling essay collection, *The Good Immigrant*, which won the reader's choice at the Books Are My Bag Awards. He is the author of three YA novels, *Run, Riot* (shortlisted for a National Book Award), *The Boxer* (longlisted for the Carnegie Medal), and *Stand Up*. Nikesh was one of Time Magazine's cultural leaders, Foreign Policy magazine's 100 Global Thinkers and The Bookseller's 100 most influential people in publishing in 2016 and in 2017. He is the co-founder of the literary journal, The Good Journal and The Good Literary Agency. Nikesh has also written a memoir, *Brown Baby: A Memoir Of Race, Family And Home* and a book on writing called, *Your Story Matters*.

ROCHELLE FALCONER

Illustrator

Rochelle was born in Jamaica but grew up in Birmingham, the oldest of six kids, raised by her single mum. As a teenager her head was always in a book. She loved to write – and at school the art department was where she felt most at home. Rochelle studied graphic design – and has worked for various design agencies as well as the gaming industry. It wasn't until she took a break to raise a family, that she rediscovered picture books. Combining her early passion for writing and her love of drawing, Rochelle now spends her time creating characters she would love to see represented in picture books, and dreaming up their stories.

KNIGHTS OF

KNIGHTS OF is a multi award-winning inclusive publisher focused on bringing underrepresented voices to the forefront of commercial children's publishing. With a team led by women of colour, and an unwavering focus on their intended readership for each book, Knights Of works to engage with gatekeepers across the industry, including booksellers, teachers and librarians, and supports non-traditional community spaces with events, outreach, marketing and partnerships.